Rules at the Library

Dwayne Hicks

illustrated by
Aurora Aguilera

PowerKiDS press

New York

Published in 2020 by The Rosen Publishing Group, Inc.
29 East 21st Street, New York, NY 10010

First Edition

Editor: Elizabeth Krajnik
Art Director: Michael Flynn
Book Design: Raúl Rodriguez
Illustrator: Aurora Aguilera

Cataloging-in-Publication Data
Names: Hicks, Dwayne, author.
Title: Rules at the library / Dwayne Hicks.
Description: New York : PowerKids Press, [2020] | Series: Rules at school |
   Includes index.
Identifiers: LCCN 2018024141| ISBN 9781538344361 (library bound) | ISBN
   9781538345665 (pbk.) | ISBN 9781538345672 (6 pack)
Subjects: LCSH: Libraries—Juvenile literature. | School libraries—Juvenile
   literature.
Classification: LCC Z665.5 .H53 2020 | DDC 027—dc23
LC record available at https://lccn.loc.gov/2018024141

Manufactured in the United States of America

CPSIA Compliance Information: Batch #CSPK19. For further information contact Rosen Publishing, New York, New York at 1-800-237-9932.

Contents

Rashid is in kindergarten.
He likes to learn!

It's time for library.
Rashid waits his turn in line.

Miss Fowler is the librarian.

"Hi, Miss Fowler!"

"Hello, Rashid!"

"Remember the rules of the library," says Miss Fowler.

8

"Don't be loud. Share with others. Clean up your messes. Have fun!"

9

First, Rashid returns a book he
borrowed from the library.

Then, he looks for another book
to borrow.

Rashid wants to play a computer game.

His friends are using the computers.
Rashid waits his turn.

Now it's Rashid's turn to use a computer.

Laura wants to play too.
"Sure," Rashid says.
"Let's play!"

"Who wants to color?" asks Miss Fowler.

Rashid shares the crayons
with Laura.

Laura tells a joke. Rashid laughs!

"You're too loud," says Miss Fowler.
"Sorry," says Rashid.

It's time to clean up.

Rashid helps.

He puts the crayons away.

Library is Rashid's favorite
part of school. Rashid knows
the rules of the library.

23

Words to Know

book

computer

crayons

Index